Tom Taylor

Our American Cousin

Outlook

Tom Taylor

Our American Cousin

1. Auflage | ISBN: 978-3-73262-756-1

Erscheinungsort: Frankfurt am Main, Deutschland

Erscheinungsjahr: 2018

Outlook Verlag GmbH, Frankfurt.

OUR AMERICAN COUSIN

A Drama, in 3 Acts.

By Tom Taylor

OUR AMERICAN COUSIN.

ACT I.

Scene 1—Drawing room in 3. Trenchard Manor, C. D., backed by interior, discovering table with luncheon spread. Large French window, R. 3 E., through which a fine English park is seen. Open archway, L. 3 E. Set balcony behind. Table, R., books and papers on it. Work basket containing wools and embroidery frame. A fashionable arm chair and sofa, L. 2 E., small table near C. D. Stage handsomely set, costly furniture, carpet down, chairs, etc.

Buddicombe discovered on sofa reading newspaper. Skillet and Sharpe busily arranging furniture as curtain rises.

Sharpe I don't know how you may feel as a visitor, Mr. Buddicombe, but I think this is a most uncomfortable family.

Bud Very uncomfortable. I have no curtain to my bed.

Skil And no wine at the second table.

Sharpe And meaner servants I never seed.

Bud I'm afraid Sir Edward is in a queer strait.

Skil Yes, for only this morning, Mr. Binny, Mrs. Skillet says he—

Enter Binny, L. 3 E.

Binny Mind your hown business instead hof your betters. I'm disgusted with you lower servants. When the wine merchant presents his bills, you men, hear me, say he's been pressing for the last six months, do you?

Skil Nor I, that the last year's milliner's bills have not been paid.

Sharpe Nor I, that Miss Florence has not had no new dresses from London all winter.

Bud And I can solemnly swear that his lordship's hair has been faithfully bound in this bosom.

Binny That'll do, that'll do; but to remember to check hidle curiosity is the first duty of men hin livery. Ha, 'ere hare the letters.

Enter John Wickens, L. 3 E., with green baize bag. Binny takes bag, takes out letters and reads addresses.

Binny Hah! bill, of course, Miss Augusta, Mrs. Mountchessington, Lord

Dundreary, Capt. De Boots, Miss Georgina Mountchessington, Lieut. Vernon, ah! that's from the admiralty. What's this? Miss Florence Trenchard, via Brattleboro', Vermont.

Bud Where's that, Mr. Binny.

John Why that be hin the United States of North Hamerica, and a main good place for poor folks.

Binny John Wickens, you forget yourself.

John Beg pardon, Mr. Binny.

Binny John Wickens, leave the room.

John But I know where Vermont be tho'.

Binny John Wickens, get hout. [Exit John, L. 3 E.]

Bud Dreadful low fellow, that.

Binny Halways himpudent.

Bud [Looking at letter in Binny's hand.] Why, that is Sir Edward's hand, Mr. Binny, he must have been sporting.

Binny Yes, shooting the wild helephants and buffalos what abound there.

Bud The nasty beasts. [Looking off, R. 2 E.] Hello, there comes Miss Florence tearing across the lane like a three year old colt.

Sharp & **Skil** Oh, Gemini. [Run off, R. 2 E. Bud. runs off, L. 2 E.]

Enter Florence, R. 2 E.

Flo [As if after running.] Oh! I'm fairly out of breath. Good morning, Binny, the letter bag I saw coming, Wickens coming with it. I thought I could catch him before I reached the house. [Sits R.] So off I started, I forgot the pond, it was in or over. I got over, but my hat got in. I wish you'd fish it out for me, you won't find the pond very deep.

Binny Me fish for an at? Does she take me for an hangler?

Flo. Give me the letters. [Takes them.] Ah, blessed budget that descends upon Trenchard Manor, like rain on a duck pond. Tell papa and all, that the letters have come, you will find them on the terrace.

Binny Yes, Miss. [Going, L. 3 E.]

Flo And then go fish out my hat out of the pond, it's not very deep Binny [Aside.] Me fish for 'ats? I wonder if she takes me for an hangler? [Exit disgusted, R. 3 E.]

Flo [Reading directions.] Lieut. Vernon. [This is a large letter with a large white envelope, red seal.] In her Majesty's service. Admiralty, R. N. Ah, that's an answer to Harry's application for a ship. Papa promised to use his influence for him. I hope he has succeeded, but then he will have to leave us, and who knows if he ever comes back. What a foolish girl I am, when I know that his rise in the service will depend upon it. I do hope he'll get it, and, if he must leave us, I'll bid him good bye as a lass who loves a sailor should.

Enter Sir Edward, Mrs. M., Augusta, Capt. De Boots, Vernon, L. 3 E.

Flo Papa, dear, here are letters for you, one for you, Mrs. Mountchessington, one for you, Capt. De Boots, and one for you, Harry. [Hiding letter behind her.]

Ver Ah, one for me, Florence?

Flo Now what will you give me for one?

Ver Ah, then you have one?

Flo Yes, there, Harry. [Gives it.]

Ver Ah, for a ship. [Opens and reads.]

Flo Ah! Mon ami, you are to leave us. Good news, or bad?

Ver No ship yet, this promises another year of land lubbery. [Goes up.]

Flo. I'm so sorry. [Aside.] I'm so glad he's not going away. But where's Dundreary. Has anybody seen Dundreary?

Enter Dundreary.

Dun Good morning, Miss Florence.

Flo [Comes down, L.] Good morning, my Lord Dundreary. Who do you think has been here? What does the postman bring?

Dun Well, sometimes he brings a bag with a lock on it, sometimes newspapers, and sometimes letters, I suppothe.

Flo There. [Gives letter. Dundreary opens letter and Florence goes up R. Dun. knocks knees against chair, turns round knocks shins, and at last is seated extreme, R.]

Dun Thank you. [Reads letter.]

De B [Reading paper.] By Jove, old Soloman has made a crop of it.

Dun A—what of it?

De B I beg pardon, an event I am deeply interested in, that's all. I beg pardon.

Aug Ah! Florence, dear, there's a letter of yours got among mine. [Gives it.]

Flo Why papa, it's from dear brother Ned.

Sir E From my boy! Where is he? How is he? Read it.

Flo He writes from Brattleboro' Vt. [Reading written letter.] "Quite well, just come in from a shooting excursion, with a party of Crows, splendid fellows, six feet high."

Dun Birds six feet high, what tremendous animals they must be.

Flo Oh, I see what my brother means; a tribe of indians called Crows, not birds.

Dun Oh, I thought you meant those creatures with wigs on them.

Flo Wigs!

Dun I mean those things that move, breathe and walk, they look like animals with those things. [Moving his arms like wings.]

Flo Wings.

Dun Birds with wings, that's the idea.

Flo [Reading written letter.] "Bye-the-bye, I have lately come quite hap-hazard upon the other branch of our family, which emigrated to America at the Restoration. They are now thriving in this State, and discovering our relationship, they received me most hospitably. I have cleared up the mysterious death of old Mark Trenchard."

Sir E Of my uncle!

Flo [Reading written letter.] "It appears that when he quarreled with his daughter on her marriage with poor Meredith, he came here in search of this stray shoot of the family tree, found them and died in their house, leaving Asa, one of the sons, heir to his personal property in England, which ought to belong to poor Mary Meredith. Asa is about to sail for the old country, to take possession. I gave him directions to find you out, and he should arrive almost as soon as this letter. Receive him kindly for the sake of the kindness he has shown to me, and let him see some of our shooting." Your affectionate brother, NED.

Sir E An American branch of the family.

Mrs M Oh, how interesting!

Aug [Enthusiastically.] How delightfully romantic! I can imagine the wild young hunter. An Apollo of the prairie.

Flo An Apollo of the prairie; yes, with a strong nasal twang, and a decided taste for tobacco and cobblers.

Sir E Florence, you forget that he is a Trenchard, and no true Trenchard would have a liking for cobblers or low people of that kind.

Flo I hate him, whatever he is, coming here to rob poor cousin Mary of her grandmother's guineas.

Sir E Florence, how often must I request you not to speak of Mary Meredith as your cousin?

Flo Why, she is my cousin, is she not? Besides she presides over her milk pail like a duchess playing dairymaid. [Sir E. goes up.] Ah! Papa won't hear me speak of my poor cousin, and then I'm so fond of syllabubs. Dundreary, do you know what syllabubs are?

Dun Oh, yeth, I know what syllabubs is—yeth—yeth.

Flo Why, I don't believe you do know what they are.

Dun Not know what syllabubs are? That's a good idea. Why they are—syllabubs are—they are only babies, idiotic children; that's a good idea, that's good. [Bumps head against Florence.]

Flo No, it's not a bit like the idea. What you mean are called cherubims.

Dun What, those things that look like oranges, with wings on them?

Flo Not a bit like it. Well, after luncheon you must go with me and I'll introduce you to my cousin Mary and syllabubs.

Dun I never saw Mr. Syllabubs, I am sure.

Flo Well, now, don't forget.

Dun I never can forget—when I can recollect.

Flo Then recollect that you have an appointment with me after luncheon.

Dun Yeth, yeth.

Flo Well, what have you after luncheon?

Dun Well, sometimes I have a glass of brandy with an egg in it, sometimes a run ‘round the duck-pond, sometimes a game of checkers—that’s for exercise, and perhaps a game of billiards.

Flo No, no; you have with me after luncheon, an ap—an ap—

Dun An ap— an ap—

Flo An ap—an appoint—appointment.

Dun An ointment, that’s the idea. [Knocks against De Boots as they go up stage.]

Mrs M [Aside.] That artful girl has designs upon Lord Dundreary. Augusta, dear, go and see how your poor, dear sister is this morning.

Aug Yes, mamma. [Exit, L. 1 E.]

Mrs M She is a great sufferer, my dear.

Dun Yeth, but a lonely one.

Flo What sort of a night had she?

Mrs M Oh, a very refreshing one, thanks to the draught you were kind enough to prescribe for her, Lord Dundreary.

Flo What! Has Lord Dundreary been prescribing for Georgina?

Dun Yeth. You see I gave her a draught that cured the effect of the draught, and that draught was a draft that didn’t pay the doctor’s bill. Didn’t that draught—

Flo Good gracious! what a number of draughts. You have almost a game of draughts.

Dun Ha! ha! ha!

Flo What’s the matter?

Dun That wath a joke, that wath.

Flo Where's the joke? [Dundreary screams and turns to Mrs. M.]

Mrs M No.

Dun She don't see it. Don't you see—a game of drafts—pieces of wound wood on square pieces of leather. That's the idea. Now, I want to put your brains to the test. I want to ask you a whime.

Flo A whime, what's that?

Dun A whime is a widdle, you know.

Flo A widdle!

Dun Yeth; one of those things, like—why is so and so or somebody like somebody else.

Flo Oh, I see, you mean a conundrum.

Dun Yeth, a drum, that's the idea. What is it gives a cold in the head, cures a cold, pays the doctor's bill and makes the home-guard look for substitutes? [Florence repeats it.] Yeth, do you give it up?

Flo Yes.

Dun Well, I'll tell you—a draught. Now I've got a better one that that: When is a dog's tail not a dog's tail? [Florence repeats. During this Florence, Mrs. M. and Dundreary are down stage.]

Flo Yes, and willingly.

Dun When it's a cart. [They look at him enquiringly.]

Flo Why, what in earth has a dog's tail to do with a cart?

Dun When it moves about, you know. A horse makes a cart move, so does a dog make his tail move.

Flo Oh, I see what you mean—when it's a wagon. [Wags the letter in her hand.]

Dun Well, a wagon and a cart are the same thing, ain't they! That's the idea—it's the same thing.

Flo They are not the same. In the case of your conundrum there's a very great difference.

Dun Now I've got another. Why does a dog waggle his tail?

Flo Upon my word, I never inquired.

Dun Because the tail can't waggle the dog. Ha! Ha!

Flo Ha! ha! Is that your own, Dundreary?

Dun Now I've got one, and this one is original.

Flo No, no, don't spoil the last one.

Dun Yeth; but this is extremely interesting.

Mrs M Do you think so, LordDundreary?

Dun Yeth. Miss Georgina likes me to tell her my jokes. Bye-the-bye, talking of that lonely sufferer, isn't she an interesting invalid? They do say that's what's the matter with me. I'm an interesting invalid.

Flo Oh, that accounts for what I have heard so many young ladies say—Florence, dear, don't you think Lord Dundreary's extremely interesting? I never knew what they meant before.

Dun Yeth, the doctor recommends me to drink donkey's milk.

Flo [Hiding laugh.] Oh, what a clever man he must be. He knows we generally thrive best on our native food. [Goes up.]

Dun [Looking first at Florence and then at Mrs M.] I'm so weak, and that is so strong. Yes, I'm naturally very weak, and I want strengthening. Yes, I guess I'll try it.

Enter Augusta. Bus. with Dundreary, who finally exits and brings on Georgina, L. 1 E.

Dun Look at this lonely sufferer. [Bringing on Georgina, seats her on sofa, L.] There, repothe yourself.

Geo [Fanning herself] Thank you, my lord. Everybody is kind to me, and I am so delicate.

Aug [At table.] Capt. De Boots, do help to unravel these wools for me, you have such an eye for color.

Flo An eye for color! Yes, especially green.

Dun [Screams.] Ha! ha! ha!

All What's the matter?

Dun Why, that wath a joke, that wath.

Flo Where was the joke?

Dun Especially, ha! ha!

Sir E Florence, dear, I must leave you to represent me to my guests. These letters will give me a great deal of business to-day.

Flo Well, papa, remember I am your little clerk and person of all work.

Sir E No, no; this is private business—money matters, my love, which women know nothing about. [Aside.] Luckily for them, I expect Mr. Coyle to-day.

Flo Dear papa, how I wish you would get another agent.

Sir E Nonsense, Florence, impossible. He knows my affairs. His father was agent for the late Baronet. He's one of the family, almost.

Flo Papa, I have implicit faith in my own judgement of faces. Depend upon it, that man is not to be trusted.

Sir E Florence, you are ridiculous. I could not get on a week without him. [Aside.] Curse him, I wish I could! Coyle is a most intelligent agent, and a most faithful servant of the family.

Enter Binny, L. 3 E.

Binny Mr. Coyle and hagent with papers.

Sir E Show him into the library. I will be with him presently. [Exit Binny.]

Flo Remember the archery meeting, papa. It is at three.

Sir E Yes, yes, I'll remember. [Aside.] Pretty time for such levity when ruin stares me in the face. Florence, I leave you as my representative. [Aside.] Now to prepare myself to meet my Shylock. [Exit, R. 1 E.]

Flo Why will papa not trust me? [Vernon comes down, R.] Oh, Harry! I wish he would find out what a lot of pluck and common sense there is in this feather head of mine.

Dun Miss Florence, will you be kind enough to tell Miss Georgina all about that American relative of yours.

Flo Oh, about my American cousin; certainly. [Aside to Harry.] Let's have some fun. Well, he's about 17 feet high!

Dun Good gracious! 17 feet high!

Flo They are all 17 feet high in America, ain't they, Mr. Vernon?

Ver Yes, that's about the average height.

Flo And they have long black hair that reaches down to their heels; they have dark copper-colored skin, and they fight with—What do they fight with, Mr. Vernon?

Ver Tomahawks and scalping knives.

Flo Yes; and you'd better take care, Miss Georgina, or he'll take his tomahawk and scalping knife and scalp you immediately. [Georgina screams and faints.]

Dun Here, somebody get something and throw over her; a pail of water; no, not that, she's pale enough already. [Fans her with handkerchief.] Georgina, don't be afraid. Dundreary's by your side, he will protect you.

Flo Don't be frightened, Georgina. He will never harm you while Dundreary is about. Why, he could get three scalps here. [Pulls Dundreary's whiskers. Georgina screams.]

Dun Don't scream, I won't lose my whiskers. I know what I'll do for my own safety. I will take this handkerchief and tie the roof of my head on. [Ties it on.]

Flo [Pretending to cry.] Good bye, Dundreary. I'll never see you again in all your glory.

Dun Don't cry, Miss Florence, I'm ready for Mr. Tommy Hawk.

Enter Binny.

Binny If you please, Miss, 'ere's a gent what says he's hexpected.

Flo What's his name? Where's his card?

Binny He didn't tell me his name, Miss, and when I haxed him for his card 'e said 'e had a whole pack in his valise, and if I 'ad a mine 'e'd play me a game of seven hup. He says he has come to stay, and he certainly looks as if he didn't mean to go.

Flo That's him. Show him in, Mr. Binny. [Exit Binny, L. 3 E.] That's my American cousin, I know.

Aug [Romantically.] Your American cousin. Oh, how delightfully romantic, isn't it, Capt. De Boots? [Comes down.] I can imagine the wild young hunter, with the free step and majestic mien of the hunter of the forest.

Asa [Outside, L. 3 E.] Consarn your picture, didn't I tell you I was expected? You are as obstinate as Deacon Stumps' forelock, that wouldn't lie down and couldn't stand up. Would't pint forward and couldn't go backward.

Enter Asa, L. 3 E., carrying a valise.

Asa Where's the Squire?

Flo Do you mean Sir Edward Trenchard, sir?

Asa Yes.

Flo He is not present, but I am his daughter.

Asa Well, I guess that'll fit about as well if you tell this darned old shoat to take me to my room.

Flo What does he mean by shoat?

Binny [Taking valise.] He means me, mum; but what he wants—

Asa Hurry up, old hoss!

Binny He calls me a 'oss, Miss, I suppose I shall be a hox next, or perhaps an 'ogg.

Asa Wal, darn me if you ain't the consarnedest old shoat I ever did see since I was baptized Asa Trenchard.

Flo Ah! then it is our American cousin. Glad to see you—my brother told us to expect you.

Asa Wal, yes, I guess you do b'long to my family. I'm Asa Trenchard, born in Vermont, suckled on the banks of Muddy Creek, about the tallest gunner, the slickest dancer, and generally the loudest critter in the state. You're my cousin, be you? Wal, I ain't got no objections to kiss you, as one cousin ought to kiss another.

Ver Sir, how dare you?

Asa Are you one of the family? Cause if you ain't, you've got no right to interfere, and if you be, you needn't be alarmed, I ain't going to kiss you. Here's your young man's letter. [Gives letter and attempts to kiss her.]

Flo In the old country, Mr. Trenchard, cousins content themselves with hands, but our hearts are with them. You are welcome, there is mine. [Gives her hand, which he shakes heartily.]

Asa That'll do about as well. I won't kiss you if you don't want me to; but if you did, I wouldn't stop on account of that sailor man. [Business of Vernon threatening Asa.] Oh! now you needn't get your back up. What an all-fired chap you are. Now if you'll have me shown to my room, I should like to fix up a bit and put on a clean buzzom. [All start.] Why, what on earth is the matter with you all? I only spoke because you're so all-fired go-to-meeting like.

Flo Show Mr. Trenchard to the red room, Mr. Binny, that is if you are done with it, Mr. Dundreary.

Dun Yeth, Miss Florence. The room and I have got through with each other, yeth.

[Asa and Dundreary see each other for the first time. Business of recognition, ad. lib.]

Asa Concentrated essence of baboons, what on earth is that?

Dun He's mad. Yes, Miss Florence, I've done with that room. The rooks crowed so that they racked my brain.

Asa You don't mean to say that you've got any brains.

Dun No, sir, such a thing never entered my head. The wed indians want to scalp me. [Holding hands to his head.]

Flo The red room, then, Mr. Binny.

Asa [To Binny.] Hold on! [Examines him.] Wal, darn me, but you keep your help in all-fired good order here. [Feels of him.] This old shoat is fat enough to kill. [Hits Binny in stomach. Binny runs off, L. 2 E.] Mind how you go up stairs, old hoss, or you'll bust your biler. [Exit, L. 3 E.]

Dun Now he thinks Binny's an engine and has got a boiler.

Flo Oh, what fun!

Mrs M Old Mark Trenchard died very rich, did he not,Florence?

Flo Very rich, I believe.

Aug He's not at all romantic, is he, mamma?

Mrs M [Aside to her] My dear, I have no doubt he has solid good qualities, and I don't want you to laugh at him like Florence Trenchard.

Aug No, mamma, I won't.

Flo But what are we to do with him?

Dun Ha! Ha! ha!

All What is the matter?

Dun I've got an idea.

Flo Oh! let's hear Dundreary's idea.

Dun It's so seldom I get an idea that when I do get one it startles me. Let us get a pickle bottle.

Flo Pickle bottle! [All come down.]

Dun Yeth; one of those things with glasssides.

Enter Asa, L. 2 E.

Flo Oh! you mean a glass case.

Dun Yeth, a glass case, that's the idea, and let us put this Mr. Thomas Hawk in it, and have him on exhibition. That's the idea.

Asa [Down L. of Florence, overhearing.] Oh! that's your idea, is it? Wal, stranger, I don't know what they're going to do with me, but wherever they do put me, I hope it will be out of the reach of a jackass. I'm a real hoss, I am, and I get kinder riley with those critters.

Dun Now he thinks he's a horse. I've heard of a great jackass, and I dreampt of a jackass, but I don't believe there is any such insect.

Flo Well, cousin, I hope you made yourself comfortable.

Asa Well, no, I can't say as I did. You see there was so many all-fired fixins in my room I couldn't find anything I wanted.

Flo What was it you couldn't find in your room?

Asa There as no soft soap.

De B Soft soap!

Aug Soft soap!

Ver Soft soap!

Mrs M Soft soap!

Flo Soft soap!

Geo [On sofa.] Soft soap!

Dun Thoft thoap?

Asa Yes, soft soap. I reckon you know what that is. However, I struck a pump in the kitchen, slicked my hair down a little, gave my boots a lick of grease, and now I feel quite handsome; but I'm everlastingly dry.

Flo You'll find ale, wine and luncheon on the side-table.

Asa Wal, I don't know as I've got any appetite. You see comin' along on the cars I worried down half a dozen ham sandwiches, eight or ten boiled eggs, two or three pumpkin pies and a string of cold sausages—and—Wal, I guess I can hold on till dinner-time.

Dun Did that illustrious exile eat all that? I wonder where he put it?

Asa I'm as dry as a sap-tree in August.

Binny [Throwing open, E. D.] Luncheon!

Asa [Goes hastily up to table.] Wal, I don't want to speak out too plain, but this is an awful mean set out for a big house like this.

Flo Why, what's wrong, sir?

Asa Why, there's no mush!

Asa Nary slapjack.

Dun Why, does he want Mary to slap Jack?

Asa No pork and beans!

Dun Pork's been here, but he's left.

Asa And where on airth's the clam chowder?

Dun Where *is* clam chowder? He's never here when he's wanted.

Asa [Drinks and spits.] Here's your health, old hoss. Do you call that a drink? See here, cousin, you seem to be the liveliest critter here, so just hurry up the fixins, and I'll show this benighted aristocratic society what real liquor is. So hurry up the fixins.

All Fixins?

Flo What do you mean by fixins?

Asa Why, brandy, rum, gin and whiskey. We'll make them all useful.

Flo Oh, I'll hurry up the fixins. What fun! [Exit, R.]

Dun Oh! I thought he meant the gas fixins.

Asa Say, you, you Mr. Puffy, you run out and get me a bunch of mint anda bundle of straws; hurry up, old hoss. [Exit Binny, L. 3 E., indignantly.] Say, Mr. Sailor man, just help me down with this table. Oh! don't you get riley, you and I ran against each other when I came in, but we'll be friends yet. [Vernon helps him with table to C.]

Enter Florence, followed by servants in livery; they carry a case of decanters and water, on which are seven or eight glasses, two or three tin mixers and a bowl of sugar. Binny enters with a bunch of mint and a few straws.

Flo Here, cousin, are the fixins.

Asa That's yer sort. Now then, I'll give you all a drink that'll make you squeal. [To Binny] Here, Puffy, just shake that up, faster. I'll give that sick gal a drink that'll make her squirm like an eel on a mud bank.

Dun [Screams.] What a horrible idea. [Runs about stage.]

Flo Oh, don't mind him! That's only an American joke.

Dun A joke! Do you call that a joke? To make a sick girl squirm like a mud bank on an eel's skin?

Asa Yes, I'll give you a drink that'll make your whiskers return under your chin, which is their natural location. Now, ladies and gentlemen, what'll you have, Whiskey Skin, Brandy Smash, Sherry Cobbler, Mint Julep or Jersey Lightning?

Aug Oh, I want a Mint Julep.

De B Give me a Gin Cocktail.

Flo I'll take a Sherry Cobbler.

Ver Brandy Smash for me.

Mrs M Give me a Whiskey Skin.

Geo I'll take a Lemonade.

Dun Give me a Jersey Lightning.

Asa Give him a Jersey Lightning. [As Dundreary drinks] Warranted to kill at forty rods. [Dundreary falls back on Mrs. M. and Georgina.]

Closed In.

Scene 2—Library in Trenchard Manor. Oriel Window, L. C., with curtains. Two chairs and table brought on at change.

Enter Binny and Coyle, L. 1 E.

Binny Sir Hedward will see you directly, Mr. Coyle.

Coyle Very well. House full of company, I see, Mr. Binny.

Binny Cram full, Mr. Coyle. As one of the first families in the country we must keep up our position.

Coyle [Rubbing his hands.] Certainly, certainly, that is as long as we can, Mr. Binny. Tell Murcott, my clerk, to bring my papers in here. You'll findhim in the servant's hall, and see that you keep your strong ale out of his way. People who serve me must have their senses about them.

Binny [Aside.] I should say so, or 'e'd 'ave hevery tooth hout in their 'eds, the wiper. [Exit, L. 1 E.]

Coyle And now to show this pompous baronet the precipice on which he stands.

Enter Murcott, with green bag and papers.

Coyle Are you sober, sirrah?

Murcott Yes, Mr. Coyle.

Coyle Then see you keep so.

Mur I'll do my best, sir. But, oh! do tell them to keep liquor out of my way. I can't keep from it now, try as I will, and I try hard enough, God help me!

Coyle Pshaw! Get out those mortgages and the letters from my London agent. [Murcott takes papers from bag and places then on table. Coyle looks off, R. 1 E.] So; here comes Sir Edward. Go, but be within call. I may want you to witness a signature.

Mur I will sir. [Aside.] I must have brandy, or my hand will not be steady enough to write. [Exit, L. 1 E.]

Enter Sir Edward, R. 1 E. Coyle bows.

Sir E Good morning, Coyle, good morning. [With affected ease.] There is a chair, Coyle. [They sit.] So you see those infernal tradespeople are pretty troublesome.

Coyle My agent's letter this morning announces that Walter and Brass have got judgement and execution on their amount for repairing your town house last season. [Refers to papers.] Boquet and Barker announce their intention of taking this same course with the wine account. Handmarth is preparing for a settlement of his heavy demand for the stables. Then there is Temper for pictures and other things and Miss Florence Trenchard's account with Madame Pompon, and—

Sir E Confound it, why harass me with details, these infernal particulars? Have you made out the total?

Coyle Four thousand, eight hundred and thirty pounds, nine shillings and sixpence.

Sir E Well, of course we must find means of settling this extortion.

Coyle Yes, Sir Edward, if possible.

Sir E If possible?

Coyle I, as your agent, must stoop to detail, you must allow me to repeat, if possible.

Sir E Why, you don't say there will be any difficulty in raising the money?

Coyle What means would you suggest, Sir Edward.

Sir E That, sir, is your business.

Coyle A foretaste in the interest on the Fanhille & Ellenthrope mortgages, you are aware both are in the arrears, the mortgagees in fact, write here to announce their intentions to foreclose. [Shows papers.]

Sir E Curse your impudence, pay them off.

Coyle How, Sir Edward?

Sir E Confound it, sir, which of us is the agent? Am I to find you brains for your own business?

Coyle No, Sir Edward, I can furnish the brains, but what I ask of you is to furnish the money.

Sir E There must be money somewhere, I came into possession of one of the finest properties in Hampshire only twenty-six years ago, and now you mean to tell me I cannot raise 4,000 pounds?

Coyle The fact is distressing, Sir Edward, but so it is.

Sir E There's the Ravensdale property unencumbered.

Coyle There, Sir Edward, you are under a mistake. The Ravensdale property is deeply encumbered, to nearly its full value.

Sir E [Springing up.] Good heavens.

Coyle I have found among my father's papers a mortgage of that very property to him.

Sir E To your father! My father's agent?

Coyle Yes, bearing date the year after the great contested election for the county, on which the late Sir Edward patriotically spent sixty thousand pounds for the honor of not being returned to Parliament.

Sir E A mortgage on the Ravensdale estate. But it must have been paid off, Mr. Coyle, [anxiously,] have you looked for the release or the receipt?

Coyle Neither exists. My father's sudden death explains sufficiently. Iwas left in ignorance of the transaction, but the seals on the deed and the stamps are intact, here it is, sir. [Shows it.]

Sir E Sir, do you know that if this be true I am something like a beggar, and your father something like a thief.

Coyle I see the first plainly, Sir Edward, but not the second.

Sir E Do you forget sir, that your father was a charity boy, fed, clothed by my father?

Coyle Well, Sir Edward?

Sir E And do you mean to tell me, sir, that your father repaid that kindness by robbing his benefactor?

Coyle Certainly not, but by advancing money to that benefactor when he wanted it, and by taking the security of one of his benefactor's estates, as any prudent man would under the circumstances.

Sir E Why, then, sir, the benefactor's property is yours. Coyle Pardon me, the legal estate you have your equity of redemption. You have only to pay the money and the estate is yours as before.

Sir E How dare you, sir, when you have just shown me that I cannot raise five hundred pounds in the world. Oh! Florence, why did I not listen to you when you warned me against this man?

Coyle [Aside.] Oh! she warned you, did she? [Aloud.] I see one means, at least, of keeping the Ravensdale estate in the family.

Sir E What is it?

Coyle By marrying your daughter to the mortgagee.

Sir E To you?

Coyle I am prepared to settle the estate on Miss Trenchard the day she becomes Mrs. Richard Coyle.

Sir E [Springing up.] You insolent scoundrel, how dare you insult me in my own house, sir. Leave it, sir, or I will have you kicked out by my servants.

Coyle I never take an angry man at his word, Sir Edward. Give a few moments reflection to my offer, you can have me kicked out afterwards.

Sir E [Pacing stage.] A beggar, Sir Edward Trenchard a beggar, see my children reduced to labor for their bread, to misery perhaps; but the alternative, Florence detests him, still the match would save her, at least, from ruin. He might take the family name, I might retrench, retire, to the continent for a few years. Florence's health might serve as a pretence. Repugnant as the alternative is, yet it deserves consideration.

Coyle [Who has watched.] Now, Sir Edward, shall I ring for the servants to kick me out?

Sir E Nay Mr. Coyle, you must pardon my outburst, you know I am hasty, and——

Flo [Without.] Papa, dear! [Enters gaily, starts on seeing Coyle.] Papa, pardon my breaking in on business, but our American cousin has come, such an original—and we are only waiting for you to escort us to the field.

Sir E I will come directly, my love. Mr. Coyle, my dear, you did not see him.

Flo [Disdainfully.] Oh! yes, I saw him, papa.

Sir E Nay, Florence, your hand to Mr. Coyle. [Aside.] I insist.

Flo Papa. [Frightened at his look, gives her hand. Coyle attempts to kiss it, she snatches it away and crosses to L.]

Sir E [Crosses to L.] Come, Florence. Mr. Coyle, we will join you in the park. Come, my love, take my arm. [Hurries her off, L. 1 E.]

Coyle Shallow, selfish fool. She warned you of me did she? And you did not heed her; you shall both pay dearly. She, for her suspicions, and you that you did not share them. [Walks up and down.] How lucky the seals were not cut from that mortgage, when the release was given. 'Tis like the silly security of the Trenchard's. This mortgage makes Ravensdale mine, while the release that restores it to its owner lies in the recess of the bureau, whose secret my father revealed to me on his death bed. [Enter Murcott, L. 1 E.] Write to the mortgagee of the Fanhill and Ellenthrope estates, to foreclose before the week is out, and tell Walters and Brass to put in execution to-day. We'll prick this wind-bag of a Baronet. Abel, we have both a bone to pick with him and his daughter. [Murcott starts.] Why, what's the matter?

Mur Nothing, the dizziness I've had lately.

Coyle Brandy in the evening, brandy in the morning, brandy all night. What a fool you are, Murcott.

Mur Who knows that as well as I do?

Coyle If you would but keep the money out of your mouth, there's the making of a man in you yet.

Mur No, no, it's gone too far, it's gone too far, thanks to the man who owns this house, you know all about it. How he found me a thriving, sober lad, flogging the village children through their spelling book. How he took a fancy to me as he called it, and employed me here to teach his son and Miss Florence. [His voice falters.] Then remember how I forgot who and what I was, and was cuffed out of the house like a dog. How I lost my school, my good name, but still hung about the place, they all looked askance at me, you don't know how that kills the heart of a man, then I took to drink and sank down, down, till I came to this.

Coyle You owe Sir Edward revenge, do you not? You shall have a rare revenge on him, that mortgage you found last week puts the remainder of the property in my reach, and I close my hand on it unless he will consent to my terms.

Mur You can drive a hard bargain. I know.

Coyle And a rare price I ask for his forbearance, Abel—his daughter's hand.

Mur Florence?

Coyle Yes, Florence marries Richard Coyle. Richard Coyle steps into Sir Edward's estates. There, you dog, will not that be a rare revenge. So follow me with those papers. [Crosses to L.] And now to lay the mine that will topple over the pride of the Trenchards. [Exit L. 1 E.]

Mur He marry Florence! Florence Trenchard! My Florence. Mine! Florence *his wife*. No, no, better a thousand times she had been mine, low as I am, when I dreampt that dream, but it shan't be, it shan't be. [Tremblingly putting papers in bag.] If I can help her, sot though I am. Yes, I can help her, if the shock don't break me down. Oh! my poor muddled brain, surely there was a release with it when I found it. I must see Florence to warn her and expose Coyle's villainy. Oh! how my poor head throbs when I try to. I shall die if I don't have a drop of brandy, yes brandy. [Exit, L. 1 E.]

Scene 3—Chamber in 3. at Trenchard Manor. Large shower bath near R. 3 E. Toilet table with draw, L. 2 E. Small bottle in draw with red sealing wax on cork. Asa discovered seated, R. with foot on table, smoking a cigar. Valise on floor in front of him. Binny discovered standing by his side.

Asa Wal, I guess I begin to feel kinder comfortable here in this place, if it wan't for this tarnal fat critter. He don't seem to have any work to do, but swells out his big bosom like an old turkey-cock in laying time. I do wonder what he's here for? Do they think I mean to absquatulate with the spoons? [Binny attempts to take valise—Asa puts his foot on it.] Let that sweat. That's my plunder.

Binny Will you have the kindness to give me your keys, hif you please, sir?

Asa What do you want with my keys?

Bin To put your things away in the wardrobe, sir.

Asa Wal, I calculate if my two shirts, three bosoms, four collars, and two pair of socks were to get into that everlasting big bunk, they'd think themselves so all-fired small I should never be able to crawl into them again.

Bin Will you take a baath before you dress?

Asa Take a baath?

Bin A baath.

Asa I suppose you mean a bath. Wal, man, I calkalate I ain't going to expose myself to the shakes by getting into cold water in this cruel cold climate of yours, so make tracks.

Bin Make what?

Asa Vamose!

Bin Make vamose!

Asa Absquatulate.

Bin Ab— what sir?

Asa Skedaddle.

Bin Skedaddle?

Asa Oh! get out.

Bin Oh! [Going.] If you are going to dress you'll want some hassistance.

Asa Assistance! what to get out of my unmentionables and into them again? Wal, 'spose I do, what then?

Bin Just ring the bell, hi'll hattend you.

Asa All right, come along. [Binny going.] Hold on, say, I may want to yawn presently and I shall want somebody to shut my mouth. [Binny hurries off, L. 1 E.] Wal, now I am alone, I can look about me and indulge the enquiring spirit of an American citizen. What an everlasting lot of things and fixins there is to be sure. [Opens table draw.] Here's a place will hold my plunder beautifully. [Sees bottle.] Hallo, what's this? [Comes down.] Something good to drink. [Smells bottle.] It smells awful bad. [Reads label.] Golden Fluid, one application turns the hair a beautiful brown, several applications will turn the hair a lustrous black. Well, if they keep on it may turn a pea green. I reckon this has been left here by some fellow who is ashamed of the natural color of his top knot. [Knock.] Come in.

Enter Binny, L. 1 E.

Bin Mr. Buddicombe, sir, my lord's hown man.

Asa Roll him in. [Binny beckons, enter Buddicombe.] Turkey cock number two, what is it?

Bud My Lord Dundreary's compliments and *have* you seen a small *bottle* in the toilet table drawer?

Asa Suppose I had, what then?

Bud My lord wants it particly.

Asa Was it a small bottle?

Bud A small bottle.

Bin Bottle small.

Asa Blue label?

Bin Label blue.

Asa Red sealing wax on the top?

Bud Red sealing wax.

Bin Wax red.

Asa Nice little bottle?

Bin Little bottle nice.

Asa Wal, I ain't seen it. [Aside.] If my lord sets a valley on it, guess it must be worth something.

Bud Sorry to trouble you, sir.

Bin [Aside to **Bud**.] What his hit?

Bud My lord's hair dye, the last bottle, and he turns red tomorrow. [Exit in haste.]

Bin Orrable, what an hawful situation, to be sure.

Asa [Aside.] So I've got my ring on that lord's nose, and if I don't make him dance to my tune it's a pity.

Bin Miss Florence begged me to say she had borrowed a costume for you, for the harchery meeting, sir.

Asa Hain't you dropped something?

Bin Where?

Asa What do you mean by the harchery meeting?

Bin Where they shoot with bows and harrows.

Asa There goes another of them, oh! you need'nt look for them, you can't find 'em when you want 'em. Now you just take my compliments to Miss Trenchard when I goes out shooting with injurious weapons I always wears my own genuine shooting costume. That's the natural buff tipped off with a little red paint.

Bin Good gracious, he'd look like Hadam and Heve, in the garden of Eden. [Exit Binny.]

Asa Wal, there's a queer lot of fixings. [Sees shower bath.] What on airth is that? Looks like a 'skeeter net, only it 'ain't long enough for a feller to lay down in unless he was to coil himself up like a woodchuck in a knot hole. I'd just like to know what the all-fired thing is meant for. [Calls.] Say Puffy, Puffy, Oh! he told me if I wanted him to ring the bell. [Looks round room.] Where on airth is the bell? [Slips partly inside shower bath, pulls rope, water comes down.] Murder! help! fire! Water! I'm drown.

Enter Skillet, **Sharpe**, R. 1 E. Binny, Buddicombe, L. 1 E., seeing Asa, all laugh, and keep it up till curtain falls.

CURTAIN.

ACT II

Scene 1.—Oriel Chamber in one.

Enter Mrs. Mountchessington and Augusta, L. 1 E., dressed for Archery Meeting.

Mrs M No, my dear Augusta, you must be very careful. I don't by any means want you to give up De Boots, his expectations are excellent, but, pray be attentive to this American savage, as I rather think he will prove the better match of the two, if what I hear of Mark Trenchard's property be correct.

Aug [Disdainfully.] Yes, ma.

Mrs M And look more cheerful, my love.

Aug I am so tired, ma, of admiring things I hate.

Mrs. M Yes, my poor love, yet we must all make sacrifices to society. Look at your poor sister, with the appetite.

Aug What am I to be enthusiastic about with that American, Ma?

Mrs M Oh! I hardly know yet, my dear. We must study him. I think ifyou read up Sam Slick a little, it might be useful, and just dip into Bancroft's History of the United States, or some of Russell's Letters; you should know something of George Washington, of whom the Americans are justly proud.

Aug Here he comes, ma. What a ridiculous figure he looks in that dress, ha! ha!

Mrs M Hush, my dear!

Enter Asa, in Archery Dress.

Aug Oh, Mr. Trenchard, why did you not bring me one of those lovely Indian's dresses of your boundless prairie?

Mrs M Yes, one of those dresses in which you hunt the buffalo.

Aug [Extravagantly.] Yes, in which you hunt the buffalo.

Asa [Imitating.] In which I hunt the buffalo. [Aside.] Buffaloes down in Vermont. [Aloud.] Wal, you see, them dresses are principally the nateral skin, tipped off with paint, and the indians object to parting with them.

Both Ahem! ahem!

Asa The first buffalo I see about here I shall hunt up for you.

Mrs M Oh, you Americans are so clever, and so acute.

Aug Yes, so 'cute.

Asa Yes, we're 'cute, we are; know soft solder when we see it.

Aug [Aside.] Ma, I do believe he's laughing at us.

Mrs M Oh, no, my dear, you are mistaken. Oh! I perceive they are appearing for the archery practice. I suppose we shall see you on the ground, Mr. Trenchard.

Asa Yes, I'll be there like a thousand of brick.

Aug A thousand of brick!

Mrs M Hush, my dear! that is doubtless some elegant American expression. Au revoir, Mr. Trenchard.

Asa Which?

Mrs M Au revoir. [Exit with Augusta, R.]

Asa No, thank you, don't take any before dinner. No use their talking Dutch to me. Wal, I never see an old gal stand fire like that, she's a real old bison bull. I feel all-fired tuckered out riding in those keers. I'd like to have a snooze if I could find a place to lay down in. [Sees curtain on window, L. E.] Oh, this might do! [Pulls curtain, then starts back.] No you don't! One shower bath a day is enough for me. [Cautiously opens them.] No, I guess this is all right, I shall be just as snug in here as in a pew at meeting, or a private box at the Theatre. Hello! somebody's coming. [Goes into recess.]

Enter Dundreary and Buddicombe, L. 1 E.

Bud My lord—

Dun [Business.]

Bud My lord!

Dun [Business.]

Bud Your lordship!! [Louder.]

Dun There, now you've spoiled it.

Bud Spoiled what, my lord?

Dun Spoiled what, my lord; why, a most magnificent sneeze!

Bud I am very sorry, my lord.

Dun Now that I can speak alone with you, tell me about that hair dye. Have you found it?

Bud Not a trace of it, my lord.

Dun If you don't find it, I'll discharge you.

Bud Very well, my lord. [Bows and exits, L. 1 E.]

Dun Very well, my lord! He's gone and lost my hair dye, and my hair turns red to-morrow, and when I ask him to find it for me or I'll discharge him, he says, "Very well, my lord." He's positively idiotic, he is— Ah! here comes Miss Georgina, that gorgeous creature—that lovely sufferer. [Exit, L. 1 E.]

Asa [Looking out.] What's the price of hair dye? Hallo! he's coming again with that sick girl.

Re-enter Dundreary and Georgina, L. 1 E.

Dun Will you try and strengthen your limbs with a gentle walk in the garden?

Georgina No, thank you, my lord. I'm so delicate. Oh, my lord, it is so painful to walk languidly through life, to be unable, at times, to bear the perfumes of one's favorite flowers. Even those violets you sent me yesterday I was compelled to have removed from my room, the perfume was too strong for me. I'm *so* delicate.

Dun Yes, Miss Georgina; but they're very strengthening flowers, you know.

Geo Yes, my lord, you are always right.

Dun Do you know I'm getting to be very robust?

Geo Would I could share that fault with you; but I am so delicate.

DunIf you were robust I should not love you as I do. It would deprive you of that charm which enchains me to your lovely side, which—which—

Geo Oh, my lord, my lord! I'm going to faint.

Dun And I'm going to sneeze, you faint while I sneeze.

Geo [Taking his arm.] Oh! my lord.

Dun Do you know what a sneeze is?

Geo No, my lord.

Dun She never sneezed. I'll tell you what a sneeze is. Imagine a very large spider.

Geo [Screams.] Where, my lord?

Dun No, no, I don't mean a real spider, only an imaginary one, a large spider getting up your nose, and all of a sudden, much to his disgust, he discovers he has put his foot in it and can't get it out again.

Geo That must be very distressing.

Dun For the spider, yes, and not very pleasant for the nose.

Geo Oh! my lord, do take me to mamma.

Dun No, you lovely sufferer, let's walk a little more.

Geo I can't my lord, I'm *so* delicate.

Dun Well, then, exercise, imitate that little hop of mine. [Hops.] It isn't a run, it's a—

Geo What is it?

Dun No, it isn't a what is it. Well, let me suppose I get you an oyster. [Georgina shakes her head.] Oh! then suppose I get you an oyster.

Geo No, my lord, I'm too delicate.

Dun How would you like the left wing of a canary bird?

Geo No, my lord, it's too strong for me.

Dun Let me ask you a widdle—why does a duck go under water? for divers reasons. Now I'll give you another—why does a duck come out of the water? for sundry reasons. No! No! see, you live on suction, you're like that bird with a long bill, they call doctor, no, that's not it, I thought it was a doctor, because it has a long bill—I mean a snipe—yes, you're a lovely snipe. [Exeunt, R.]

Asa [Looking after them.] There goes a load of wooden nutmegs. Hello, here comes somebody else.

Enter Florence, R., with paper.

Flo. [Reads.] "One who still remembers what he ought long since to have forgotten, wishes to speak with Miss Trenchard." Florence scratched out, "on matters of life and death, near the orel, in the west gallery," Written upon a dirty sheet of paper, in a hardly legible hand. What does this mean; it opens like one of Mrs. Radcliffe's romances. Well, here I am, and now for my correspondent.

Enter Murcott, L.

Mur Oh! for one minute's clear head, Miss Florence.

Flo I presume you are the writer of this?

Mur Yes, I am.

Flo You address me as an old acquaintance, but I do not recognize you.

Mur So much the better. So much the better.

Flo I hate mystery, sir; but you see I have come to rendezvous. I must know to whom I am speaking.

Mur As frank as ever. I am Abel Murcott.

Flo Starting back! You?

Mur Do not be ashamed, I have not the strength to injure you, if I had the evil. In this shabby, broken down drunkard you need not fear the madman, who years ago forgot in his frantic passion the gulf that lay between your station and his own. I am harmless except to my self.

Flo Speak on, sir; I hear you.

Mur I need not tell you by what steps I came to this, you don't know, maybe you never knew, what a maddening thing a passion is when it turns against itself. After being expelled from my tutorship in this house, I lost my employment, self respect, hope. I sought to drown recollection and draw courage from drink. It only embittered remembrances, and destroyed the little courage I had left. That I have bread to eat, I owe to Mr. Coyle; he employed me as his clerk. You know he has been with your father this morning. I have come to tell you my errand; are you as brave as you used to be when I knew —

Flo I fear nothing.

Mur I come to tell you of your father's ruin, his utter ruin.

Flo My father's ruin? What? What?

Mur His estates are mortgaged, his creditors clamorous. The Bailiffs will be in Trenchard Manor to-day, disguised as your own servants. This much Mr. Coyle has conceded to your father's respect for appearances.

Flo Then beggary stares him in the face. Poor father, what a sad blow for him. Is that all, sir?

Mur No; the worst remains.

Flo Go on, sir.

Mur Coyle knows your father's weakness and as a means of escape from ruin to the verge of which he has brought him, he has this day proposed for your hand.

Flo Mine!

Mur On consideration of settling on you the Ravensdale Estate.

Flo And my father, how did he listen to such insolence?

Mur You know as well as I do how he would hear such a proposal, at first a torrent of rage, then the strong ebb of selfishness set in, and he consented to listen to the terms, to view them as something to be considered, to consider them.

Flo Good Heavens, can this be true? No, I will not believe it of my father, and from such lips.

Mur You have full right to think this and to say it, but mark your father and Coyle to-day. You will then see if I speak truth or not.

Flo Forgive my distrust, Mr. Murcott.

Mur I am past taking offence or feeling scorn, I have carried more than can be heaped upon me, but I did not come only to give you warning of your danger.

Flo Can you avert it?

Asa (Coming down between them). Wal, stranger that's just the question I was going to ask.

Flo You here, sir, and listening.

Asa Wal, it wasn't purpose, I went in there to take a snooze, I heard you talking and I thought it wouldn't be polite of me not to listen to what you had to say. I'm a rough sort of a customer, and don't know much about the ways of great folks. But I've got a cool head, a stout arm, and a willing heart, and I think I can help you, just as one cousin ought to help another.

Flo Well, I do think you are honest.

Mur Shall I go on?

Flo Yes, we will trust him, go on.

Mur I found the Ravensdale mortgage while rumaging in an old deed box of Coyle's father's, there was a folded paper inside the deed. I took both to Coyle unopened, like a besotted fool that I was. My belief is strong that the paper was the release of the mortgage that the money had been paid off, and the release executed without the seals having been cut from the original mortgage. I have known such things happen.

Asa Have ye, now? Well, if a Yankee lawyer had done such a thing he would have Judge Lynch after him in no time.

Mur You can but find that release, we may unmask this diabolical fiend and save you.

Flo But, surely, a villain of Coyle's stability would have destroyed the paper, the very key-stone of his fraud.

Mur I fear so.

Asa Do you, now, wal, you're wrong, you're both wrong. I guess you ain't either on you done much cyphering human nature. The key stone of their fraud is just the point your mighty cute rascals always leave unsecured. Come along with me, stranger, and we'll just work up this sum a little, two heads are better than one. Yours is a little muddled, but mine's pretty clear, and if I don't circumvent that old sarpint, Coyle—

Flo Well?

Asa Say I am a skunk, that's all, and that's the meanest kind of an animal. [Exit L. 1st E.]

Flo I owe you much, Mr. Murcott, more than I can ever repay.

Mur No, no, no, if you did but know the hope of seeing you has roused all the manhood that drink and misery has left me. God bless you, Miss Florence.

Flo No, you don't call me Florence as you did when I was the truant pupil and you the indulgent tutor. [Offers her hand.]

Mur No, no; for heaven's sake do not call back that time or I shall go mad! mad! mad. [Rushes off, L. 1 E., followed by Florence.]

Scene 2—Park in 4. Rural cottage, L. 1 E., adjoining which, and projecting on stage an inside view of a dairy with sloping roof, painting backing to look like milk pans. The whole scene should have a picturesque appearance. Garden fence run across back, ornamental gate or archway, R. 3 E. Pigeon house on pole near dairy, L. C. Spinning wheel inside cottage door, one or two rustic benches, R. and L.

Enter John, R. 3 E., with two milk pails on a yoke, puts them down near dairy, then looks off, R. 3 E.

John There they go, that's a bull's eye, I warrant. Dang me though, if I wouldn't rather see Miss Mary than this cock robin sports yonder, here she comes. Good morning, Miss Mary. [Enter Mary from cottage L.]

Mary Oh, Wickens, you are there. How kind of you to help me with the milk pails to-day, when all the lads and lasses have given themselves a holiday to see the shooting.

John Ah, Miss Mary, you ought to be among then, with a green hat and feather, if all had their rights.

Mary [Laughing.] Nay, ladies without a farthing in the world, ought to put aside their ladyships and make themselves: besides I'm proud of my dairy here, just help me with this troublesome fellow, steady, don't shake it, the cream is foaming so beautifully. There. [John carries pan into cottage and returns down, R.]

John Now, Miss Mary, what can I do for you?

Mary Let me see; well, really, I do believe, Wickens, I've nothing to do but amuse myself.

John Dang it, Miss, that's a pity, cos I can't help you at that, yousee.

Mary Oh! Yes, bring me out dear old Welsh nurse's spinning wheel [Exit John into cottage, L. 2 E.] by the side of which I have stood so often, a round eyed baby wondering at its whirring wheel. [Reenter John with wheel, places it near cottage, L. 2 E.] There, that will do famously. I can catch the full scent of the jessamines.

John [R. C.] Anything more, Miss Mary?

Mary No, thank you, Wickens!

John [Going.] Good morning, Miss Mary.

Mary Good morning, Wickens.

John [Returning.] Is there anything I can get for you, Miss Mary?

Mary [Spinning.] Nothing, thank you.

John Dang me if I wouldn't like to stop all day, and watch her pretty figure and run errands for her. [Exit R. 3 E., crosses behind fence.]

Mary Poor Wickens is not the only one who thinks I am a very ill-used young body. Now I don't think so. Grandfather was rich, but he must have had a bad heart, or he never could have cast off poor mamma; had he adopted me, I should never have been so happy as I am now, uncle is kind to me in his pompous, patronizing way, and dear Florence loves me like a sister, and so I am happy. I am my own mistress here, and not anybody's humble servant, I sometimes find myself singing as the birds do, because I can't help it [Song, "Maid with the milking pail," can be introduced here.]

Enter Florence and Asa through gate, R. 3 E.

Flo Come along, cousin, come along. I want to introduce you to my little cousin. [Kisses Mary.] I've brought you a visitor, Miss Mary Meredith, Mr. Asa Trenchard, our American cousin. [They shake hands.] That will do for the present. This young gentleman has carried off the prize by three successive shots in the bull's eye.

Mary I congratulate you, sir, and am happy to see you.

Asa [Shakes hands again.] Thank you, Miss.

Flo That will do for a beginning.

Asa [Aside.] And so that is Mark Trenchard's grandchild.

Mary Why have you left the archery, Florence?

Flo Because, after Mr. Asa's display, I felt in no humor for shooting, and I have some very grave business with my cousin here.

Mary You? Grave business? Why I thought you never had any graver business than being very pretty, very amiable, and very ready to be amused.

Asa Wal, Miss, I guess the first comes natural round these diggins. [Bows.]

Mary You are very polite. This is my domain, sir, and I shall be happy to show you, that is, if you understand anything about a dairy.

Flo Yes, by the way, do you understand anything about dairies in America?

Asa Wal, I guess I do know something about cow juice. [They turn to smother laugh.] Why, if it ain't all as bright and clean as a fresh washed shirt just off the clover, and is this all your doin's, Miss?

Mary Yes, sir, I milk the cows, set up the milk, superintend the churning and make the cheese.

Asa Wal, darn me if you ain't the first raal right down useful gal I've seen on this side the pond.

Flo What's that, sir? Do you want to make me jealous?

Asa Oh, no, you needn't get your back up, you are the right sort too, but you must own you're small potatoes, and few in a hill compared to a gal like that.

Flo I'm what?

Asa Small potatoes.

Flo Will you be kind enough to translate that for me, for I don't understand American yet.

Asa Yes, I'll put it in French for you, "petite pommes des terres."

Flo Ah, it's very clear now; but, cousin, do tell me what you mean by calling me small potatoes.

Asa Wal, you can sing and paint, and play on the pianner, and in your own particular circle you are some pumpkins.

Flo Some pumpkins, first I am small potatoes, and now I'm some pumpkins.

Asa But she, she can milk cows, set up the butter, make cheese, and, darn me, if them ain't what I call raal downright feminine accomplishments.

Flo I do believe you are right cousin, so Mary do allow me to congratulate you upon not being small potatoes.

Mary Well, I must look to my dairy or all my last week's milk will be spoiled. Good bye, Florence, dear. Good bye, Mr. Trenchard. Good morning, sir. [Exit into Cottage.]

Asa [Following her to door.] Good morning, Miss. I'll call again.

Flo Well, cousin, what do you think of her?

Asa Ain't she a regular snorter?

Flo A what?

Asa Wal, perhaps I should make myself more intelligable, if I said, a squeeler, and to think I'm keepin' that everlasting angel of a gal out of her fortune all along of this bit of paper here.

Flo What is that? [Takes paper from pocket.]

Asa Old Mark Trenchard's will.

Flo Don't show it to me, I don't want to look at it, the fortune should have come to Mary, she is the only relation in the direct line.

Asa Say, cousin, you've not told her that darned property was left to me, have you?

Flo Do you think I had the heart to tell her of her misfortune?

Asa Wal, darn me, if you didn't show your good sense at any rate. [Goes up to dairy.]

Flo Well, what are you doing, showing *your* good sense?

Asa Oh, you go long.

Flo Say, cousin, I guess I've got you on a string now, as I heard you say this morning.

Asa Wal, what if you have, didn't I see you casting sheep's eyes at that sailor man this morning? Ah, I reckon I've got you on a string now. Say, has he got that ship yet?

Flo No, he hasn't, though I've used all my powers of persuasion with that Lord Dundreary, and his father has so much influence with the admiralty.

Asa Wal, din't he drop like a smoked possum?

Flo There you go, more American. No, he said he was very sorry, but he couldn't.

Asa [Taking bottle out.] Oh, he did, did he? Wal, I guess he'll do his best all the same.

Flo I shall be missed at the archery grounds. Will you take me back?

Asa Like a streak of lightning. [Offers arm and takes her to dairy.]

Flo That's not the way.

Asa No, of course not. [Takes her round stage back to dairy.]

Flo Well, but where are you going now?

Asa I was just going round. I say, cousin, don't you think you could find your way back alone.

Flo Why, what do *you* want to do?

Asa Wal, I just wanted to see how they make cheese is this darned country. [Exits into dairy.]

Flo [Laughing.] And they call that man a savage; well, I only wish we had a few more such savages in England.

Dun [Without, R. 2 E.] This way, lovely sufferer.

Flo Ah, here's Dundreary.

[Dundreary enters with Georgina, places her in rustic chair, R.]

Dun There, repothe yourself.

Geo Thank you, my lord; you are so kind to me, and I am so delicate.

Flo Yes, you look delicate, dear; how is she this morning any better?

Dun When she recovers, she'll be better.

Flo I'm afraid you don't take good care of her, you are so rough.

Dun No, I'm not wruff, either. [Sings.] I'm gentle and I'm kind, I'm —— I forget the rest

Flo Well, good morning, dear—do take care of her—good day, Dundreary. [Exit through gate.]

Dun Now, let me administer to your wants. How would you like a roast chestnut?

Geo No, my lord, I'm too delicate.

Dun Well, then, a peanut; there is a great deal of nourishment in peanuts.

Geo No, thank you.

Dun Then what can I do for you?

Geo If you please, ask the dairy maid to let me have a seat in the dairy. I am afraid of the draft, here.

Dun Oh! you want to get out of the draft, do you? Well, you're not the only one that wants to escape the draft. Is that the dairy on top of that stick? [Points to pigeon house.]

Geo No, my lord, that's the pigeon house.

Dun What do they keep in pigeon houses? Oh! pigeons, to be sure; they couldn't keep donkeys up there, could they? That's the dairy, I suppothe?

Geo Yes, my lord.

Dun What do they keep indairies?

Geo Eggs, milk, butter andcheese.

Dun What's the name of that animal with a head on it? No, I don't mean that, all animals have heads. I mean those animals with something growing out of their heads.

Geo A cow?

Dun A cow growing out of his head?

Geo No, no, horns.

Dun A cow! well, that accounts for the milk and butter; but I don't see the eggs; cows don't give eggs; then there's the cheese—do you like cheese?

Geo No, my lord.

Dun Does your brother like cheese?

Geo I have no brother. I'm so delicate.

Dun She's so delicate, she hasn't got a brother. Well, if you had a brother do you think he'd like cheese?

Geo I don't know; do please take me to the dairy.

Dun Well, I will see if I can get you a broiled sardine. [Exit into dairy.]

Geo [Jumps up.] Oh! I'm so glad he's gone. I am so dreadful hungry. I should like a plate of corn beef and cabbage, eggs and bacon, or a slice of cold ham and pickles.

Dun [Outside] Thank you, thank you.

Geo [Running back to seat.] Here he comes. Oh! I am so delicate.

Enter Dundreary.

Dun I beg you pardon, Miss Georgina, but I find upon enquiry that cows don't give sardines. But I've arranged it with the dairy maid so that you can have a seat by the window that overlooks the cow house and the pig sty, and all the pretty things.

Geo I'm afraid I'm very troublesome.

Dun Yes, you're very troublesome, you are. No, I mean you're a lovely sufferer, that's the idea. [They go up to cottage door.]

Enter Asa, running against Dundreary.

Dun There's that damned rhinoceros again. [Exit into cottage, with Georgina.]

Asa There goes that benighted aristocrat and that little toad of a sick gal. [Looks off.] There he's a settling her in a chair and covering her all over with shawls. Ah! it's a caution, how these women do fix our flint for us. Here he comes. [Takes out bottle.] How are you, hair dye. [Goes behind dairy.]

Enter Dundreary.

Dun That lovely Georgina puts me in mind of that beautiful piece of poetry. Let me see how it goes. The rose is red, the violet's blue. [Asa tips his hat over his eyes.]

Dun [Repeats.]

Asa [Repeats business.]

Dun [Comes down, takes off hat, looking in it.] There must be something alive in that hat. [Goes up, and commences again.] The rose is red, the violet's blue, sugar is sweet, and so is somebody, and so is somebody else.

Asa puts yoke on Dundreary's shoulders gently. Dundreary comes down with pails.

Dun I wonder what the devil that is? [Lowers one, then the other, they trip him up.] Oh, I see, somebody has been fishing and caught a pail. [Goes hopping up stage, stumbling over against spinning wheel. Looks at yarn on stick.] Why, what a little old man. [Sees Asa.] Say, Mr. Exile, what the devil is this?

Asa That is a steam engine, and will bust in about a minute.

Dun Well, I haven't a minute to spare, so I'll not wait till it busts. [Crosses to R., knocks against private box, R. H., apologizes.]

Asa Say, whiskers, I want to ask a favor of you.

Dun [Attempts to sneeze.] Now I've got it.

Asa Wal, but say. [Dundreary's sneezing bus.]

Asa [Takes his hand.] How are you. [Squeezes it.]

Dun There, you've spoiled it.

Asa Spoiled what?

Dun Spoiled what! why a magnificent sneeze.

Asa Oh! was that what you was trying to get through you?

Dun Get through me: he's mad.

Asa Wal, now, the naked truth is—[Leans arm on Dundreary's shoulder. Bus. by Dundreary.] Oh, come now, don't be putting on airs. Say, do you know Lieut. Vernon?

Dun Slightly.

Asa Wal, what do you think of him, on an average?

Dun Think of a man on an average?

Asa Wal, I think he's a real hoss, and he wants a ship.

Dun Well if he's a real hoss, he must want a carriage.

Asa Darn me, if that ain't good.

Dun That's good.

Asa Yes, that is good.

Dun Very good.

Asa Very good, indeed, *for you*.

Dun Now I've got it. [Tries to sneeze.]

Asa Wal, now, I say. [Dundreary trying to sneeze.]

Asa What, are you at that again?

Dundreary business. Asa bites his finger. Dundreary goes up, stumbles against chair and comes down again.

Dun I've got the influenza.

Asa Got the what?

Dun He says I've got a wart. I've got the influenza.

Asa That's it exactly. I want your influence, sir, to get that ship.

Dun That's good.

Asa Yes, that's good, ain't it.

Dun Very good.

Asa Yes, darn me, if that ain't good.

Dun For you. Ha! ha! One on that Yankee.

Asa Well done, Britisher. Wal, now, about that ship?

Dun I want all my influence, sir, for my own w—w—welations. [Stammering.]

Asa Oh! you want it for your own w—w—welations. [Mimicing.]

Dun I say, sir. [Asa pretends deafness. This bus. is ad. lib.]

Asa Eh?

Dun He's hard of hearing, and thinks he's in a balloon. Mister.

Asa Eh?

Dun He thinks he can hear with his nose. I say—

Asa Eh?

Dundreary turns Asa's nose around with his thumb. Asa puts his two hands up to Dundreary's.

Dun Now he thinks he's a musical instrument. I say—

Asa What?

Dun You stutter. I'll give you a k—k—k—

Asa No you won't give me a kick.

Dun I'll give you a c—c—card to a doctor and he'll c—c—c—

Asa No he won't kick me, either.

Dun He's idiotic. I don't mean that, he'll cure you.

Asa Same one that cured you?

Dun The same.

Asa Wal, if you're cured I want to stay sick. He must be a mighty smart man.

Dun A very clever man, he is.

Asa Wal, darn me, if there ain't a physiological change taking place. Your whiskers at this moment—

Dun My whiskers!

Asa Yes, about the ends they're as black as a niggers in billing time, and near the roots they're all speckled and streaked.

Dun [Horror struck.] My whiskers speckled and streaked?

Asa [Showing bottle.] Now, this is a wonderful invention.

Dun My hair dye. My dear sir.

Asa [Squeezing his hand.] How are you?

Dun Dear Mr. Trenchard.

Puts arm on shoulder. Asa repeats Dundreary business, putting on eyeglass, hopping round the stage and stroking whiskers.

Dun He's mad, he's deaf, he squints, stammers and he's a hopper.

Asa Now, look here, you get the Lieut. a ship and I'll give you the bottle. It's a fine swap.

Dun What the devil is a swap?

Asa Well, you give me the ship, and I'll give you the bottle to boot.

Dun What do I want of your boots? I haven't got a ship about me.

Asa You'd better make haste or your whiskers will be changed again. They'll be a pea green in about a minute.

Dun [Crosses to L.] Pea green! [Exits hastily into house.]

Asa I guess I've got a ring in his nose now. I wonder how that sick gal is getting along? Wal, darn me, if the dying swallow ain't pitching into ham and eggs and home-made bread, wal, she's a walking into the fodder like a farmer arter a day's work rail splitting. I'll just give her a start. How de do, Miss, allow me to congratulate you on the return of your appetite. [Georgina scream.] Guess I've got a ring in her pretty nose now. [Looks off, R.] Hello! here comes the lickers and shooters, it's about time I took my medicine, I reckon.

Enter, from R. 2. E., Sir E., Mrs. M. Florence, Vernon, Augusta, De Boots, Wickens, Coyle, Sharpe, Binny, Skillet, Buddicombe, two servants in livery, carrying tray and glasses, a wine basket containing four bottles to represent champagne, knife to cut strings, some powerful acid in one bottle for Asa—pop sure.

Sir E Now to distribute the prizes, and drink to the health of the winner of the golden arrow.

Flo And there must stand the hero of the day. Come, kneel down.

Asa Must I kneel down?

Flo I am going to crown you Capt. of the Archers of Trenchard Manor.

Asa [Aside to Florence.] I've got the ship.

Flo No; have you?

Sir E Come, ladies and gentlemen, take from me. [Takes glasses, Starts on seeing me in livery.] Who are these strange faces?

Coyle [In his ear.] Bailiffs, Sir Edward.

Sir E Bailiffs! Florence I am lost.

[Florence supports her father. At the same moment Dundreary enters with letter and money. Georgina appears at dairy door as Dundreary comes down, L. Asa cuts string of bottle, cork hits Dundreary. General commotion as drop descends.]

ACT III.

Scene 1—Dairy set as before in Act 2d, Scene 2.

[Asa discovered on bench, R. C., whittling stick. Mary busy with milkpans in dairy.]

Asa Miss Mary, I wish you'd leave off those everlasting dairy fixings, and come and take a hand of chat along with me.

Mary What, and leave my work? Why, when you first came here, you thought I could not be too industrious.

Asa Well, I think so yet, Miss Mary, but I've got a heap to say to you, and I never can talk while you're moving about so spry among them pans, pails and cheeses. First you raise one hand and then the other, and well, it takes the gumption right our of me.

Mary [Brings sewing down.] Well, then, I'll sit here—[sits on bench with Asa, vis-a-vis.] Well now, will that do?

Asa Well, no, Miss Mary, that won't do, neither; them eyes of yourn takes my breath away.

Mary What will I do, then?

Asa Well, I don't know, Miss Mary, but, darn me, if you could do anything that wasn't so tarnal neat and handsome, that a fellow would want to keep on doing nothing else all the time.

Mary Well, then, I'll go away. [Rises.]

Asa [Stopping her.] No, don't do that, Miss Mary, for then I'll be left in total darkness. [She sits.] Somehow I feel kinder lost, if I haven't got you to talk to. Now that I've got the latitude and longitude of all them big folks, found out the length of every lady's foot, and the soft spot on everybody's head, they can't teach me nothing; but here, [Whittling.] here I come to school.

Mary Then throw away that stick, and put away your knife, like a good boy. [Throws away stick up stage.] I must cure you of that dreadful trick of whittling.

Asa Oh, if you only knew how it helps me to keep my eyes off you, Miss Mary.

Mary But you needn't keep your eyes off me.

Asa I'm afraid I must, my eyes are awful tale-tellers, and they might be saying something you wouldn't like to hear, and that might make you mad, and then you'd shut up school, and send me home feeling about as small as a tadpole with his tail bobbed off.

Mary Don't be alarmed, I don't think I will listen to any tales that your eyes may tell unless they're tales I like and ought to hear.

Asa If I thought they'd tell any other, Miss Mary, I pluck them right out and throw them in the first turnip patch I came to.

Mary And now tell me more about your home in America. Do you know I've listened to your stories until I'm half a backwoodsman's wife already?

Asa [Aside.] Wouldn't I like to make her a whole one.

Mary Yes, I can shut my eyes and almost fancy I see your home in the backwoods. There are your two sisters running about in their sunbonnets.

Asa Debby and Nan? Yes!

Mary Then I can see the smoke curling from the chimney, then men and boys working in the fields.

Asa Yes.

Mary The girls milking the cows, and everybody so busy.

Asa Yes.

Mary And then at night, home come your four big brothers from the hunt laden with game, tired and foot sore, and covered with snow.

Asa That's so.

Mary Then how we lasses bustle about to prepare supper. The fire blazes on the hearth, while your good old mother cooks the slapjacks.

Asa [Getting very excited.] Yes.

Mary And then after supper the lads and lasses go to a corn husking. The demijohn of old peach brandy is brought out and everything is so nice.

Asa I shall faint in about five minutes, Miss Mary you're a darned sight too good for this country. You ought to make tracks.

Mary Make what?

Asa Make tracks, pack up, and emigrate to the roaring old state of Vermont, and live 'long with mother. She'd make you so comfortable, and there would be sister Debby and Nab, and well, I reckon I'd be there, too.

Mary Oh! I'm afraid if I were there your mother would find the poor English girl a sad incumbrance.

Asa Oh, she ain't proud, not a mite, besides they've all seen Britishers afore.

Mary I suppose you allude to my cousin, Edward Trenchard?

Asa Well, he wan't the only one, there was the old Squire, Mark Trenchard.

Mary [Starting Aside.] My grandfather!

Asa Oh! he was a fine old hoss, as game as a bison bull, and as gray as a coon in the fall; you see he was kinder mad with his folks here, so he came over to America to look after the original branch of the family, that's our branch. We're older than the Trenchard's on this side of the water. Yes we've got the start of the heap.

Mary Tell me, Mr. Trenchard, did he never receive any letters from his daughter?

Asa Oh yes, lots of them, but the old cuss never read them, though. He chucked them in the fire as soon as he made out who they come from.

Mary [Aside.] My poor mother.

Asa You see, as nigh as we could reckon it up, she had gone and got married again his will, and that made him mad, and well, he was a queer kind of a rusty fusty old coon, and it appeared that he got older, and rustier, and fustier and coonier every fall, you see it always took him in the fall, it was too much for him. He got took down with the ague, he was so bad the doctors gave him up, and mother she went for a minister, and while she was gone the old man called me in his room, `come in, Asa, boy,' says he, and his voice rang loud and clear as a bell, `come in,' says he. Well I comed in; `sit down,' says he; well I sot down. You see I was always a favorite with the old man.
`Asa, my boy,' says he, takin' a great piece of paper, `when I die, this sheet of paper makes you heir to all my property in England'. Well, you can calculate I pricked up my ears about that time, bime-by the minister came, and I left the room, and I do believe he had a three day's fight with the devil, for that old man's soul, but he got the upper hand of satan at last, and when the minister

had gone the old man called me into his room again. The old Squire was sitting up in his bed, his face as pale as the sheet that covered him, his silken hair flowing in silvery locks from under his red cap, and the tears rolling from his large blue eyes down his furrowed cheek, like two mill streams. Will you excuse my lighting a cigar? For the story is a long, awful moveing, and I don't think I could get on without a smoke. [Strikes match.] Wal, says he to me, and his voice was not as loud as it was afore—it was like the whisper of the wind in a pine forest, low and awful. `Asa, boy,' said he, 'I feel that I've sinned in hardening my heart against my own flesh and blood, but I will not wrong the last that is left of them; give me the light,' says he. Wal I gave him the candle that stood by his bedside, and he took the sheet of paper I was telling you of, just as I might take this. [Takes will from pocket.] And he twisted it up as I might this, [Lights will,] and he lights it just this way, and he watched it burn slowly and slowly away. Then, says he, `Asa, boy that act disinherits you, but it leaves all my property to one who has a better right to it. My own daughter's darling child, Mary Meredith,' and then he smiled, sank back upon his pillow, drew a long sigh as if he felt relieved, and that was the last of poor old Mark Trenchard.

Mary Poor Grandfather. [Buries her face and sobs.]

Asa [After bus.] Wal, I guess I'd better leave her alone. [Sees half burned will.] There lies four hundred thousand dollars, if there's a cent. Asa, boy, you're a hoss. [Starts off, R. 1 C.]

Mary To me, all to me. Oh Mr. Trenchard, how we have all wronged poor grandfather. What, gone? He felt after such tidings, he felt I should be left alone—who would suspect there was such delicacy under that rough husk, but I can hardly believe the startling news—his heiress—I, the penniless orphan of an hour ago, no longer penniless, but, alas, an orphan still, [Enter Florence.] with none to share my wealth, none to love me.

Flo [Throwing arms around Mary's neck.] What treason is this, Mary, no one to love you, eh, what's the matter? You've been weeping, and I met that American Savage coming from here; he has not been rude to you?

Mary On no, he's the gentlest of human beings, but he has just told me news that has moved me strangely.

Flo What is it, love?

Mary That all grandfather's property is mine, mine, Florence, do you understand?

Flo What! he has popped, has he? I thought he would.

Mary Who do you mean?

Flo Who? Asa Trenchard, to be sure.

Mary Asa Trenchard, why, what put that in your head?

Flo Why how can Mark Trenchard's property be yours, unless you marry the legatee.

Mary The legatee? Who?

Flo Why, you know Mark Trenchard left everything to Asa.

Mary No, no, you have been misinformed.

Flo Nonsence, he showed it to me, not an hour ago on a half sheet of rough paper just like this. [Sees will.] Like this. [Picks it up.] Why this is part of it, I believe.

Mary That's the paper he lighted his cigar with.

Flo Then he lighted his cigar with 80,000 pounds. Here is old Mark Trenchard's signature.

Mary Yes, I recognize the hand.

Flo And here are the words "Asa Trenchard, in consideration of sole heir"—etc.—etc.—etc.

Mary Oh Florence, what does this mean?

Flo It means that he is a true hero, and he loves you, you little rogue. [Embraces her.]

Mary Generous man. [Hides face in Florence's bosom.]

Flo Oh, won't I convict him, now. I'll find him at once.

Runs off, R. 3 E., Mary after her calling Florence!!! Florence!!! as scene closes.

Change

Scene 2.—Chamber as before.

Enter Mrs. Montchessington, and Augusta, L. 1 E.

Mrs M Yes, my child, while Mr. De Boots and Mr. Trenchard are both here, you must ask yourself seriously, as to the state of your affections, remember, your happiness for life will depend upon the choice you make.

Aug What would you advise, mamma? You know I am always advised by you.

Mrs M Dear, obedient child. De Boots has excellent expectations, but then they are only expectations after all. This American is rich, and on the whole I think a well regulated affection ought to incline to Asa Trenchard.

Aug Very well, mamma.

Mrs M At the same time, you must be cautious, or in grasping at Asa Trenchard's solid good qualities, you may miss them, and De Boots expectations into the bargain.

Aug Oh, I will take care not to give up my hold on poor De Boots 'till I am quite sure of the American.

Mrs M That's my own girl. [Enter Asa L.] Ah, Mr. Trenchard, we were just talking of your archery powers.

Asa Wal, I guess shooting with bows and arrows is just about like most things in life, all you've got to do is keep the sun out of your eyes, look straight—pull strong—calculate the distance, and you're sure to hit the mark in most things as well as shooting.

Aug But not in England, Mr. Trenchard. There are disinterested hearts that only ask an opportunity of showing how they despise that gold, which others set such store by.

Asa Wal, I suppose there are, Miss Gusty.

Aug All I crave is affection.

Asa [Crosses to C.] Do you, now? I wish I could make sure of that, for I've been cruelly disappointed in that particular.

Mrs M Yes, but we are old friends, Mr. Trenchard, and you needn't be afraid of us.

Asa Oh, I ain't afraid of you—both on you together.

Mrs M People sometimes look a great way off, for that which is near at hand. [Glancing at Augusta and Asa alternatively.]

Asa You don't mean, Miss Gusta. [Augusta casts sheeps eyes at him.] Now, don't look at me in that way. I can't stand it, if you do, I'll bust.

Mrs M Oh, if you only knew how refreshing this ingenuousness of yours is to an old woman of the world like me.

Asa Be you an old woman of the world?

Mrs M Yes, sir.

Aug Oh yes.

Asa Well I don't doubt it in the least. [Aside.] This gal and the old woman are trying to get me on a string. [Aloud.] Wal, then, if a rough spun fellow like me was to come forward as a suitor for you daughter's hand, you wouldn't treat me as some folks do, when they find out I wasn't heir to the fortune.

Mrs M Not heir to the fortune, Mr. Trenchard?

Asa Oh, no.

Aug What, no fortune?

Asa Nary red, it all comes to their barkin up the wrong tree about the old man's property.

Mrs M Which he left to you.

Asa Oh, no.

Aug Not to you?

Asa No, which he meant to leave to me, but he thought better on it, and left it to his granddaughter Miss Mary Meredith.

Mrs M Miss Mary Meredith! Oh, I'm delighted.

Aug Delighted?

Asa Yes, you both look tickled to death. Now, some gals, and mothers would go away from a fellow when they found that out, but you don't valley fortune, Miss Gusty?

Mrs M [Aside, crosses to Aug.] My love, you had better go.

Asa You crave affection, *you* do. Now I've no fortune, but I'm filling over with affections which I'm ready to pour out all over you like apple sass, over roast pork.

Mrs M Mr. Trenchard, you will please recollect you are addressing my daughter, and in my presence.

Asa Yes, I'm offering her my heart and hand just as she wants them with nothing in 'em.

Mrs M Augusta, dear, to your room.

Aug Yes, ma, the nasty beast. [Exit R.]

Mrs M I am aware, Mr. Trenchard, you are not used to the manners of good society, and that, alone, will excuse the impertinence of which you have been guilty.

Asa Don't know the manners of good society, eh? Well, I guess I know enough to turn you inside out, old gal—you sockdologizing old man-trap. Wal, now, when I think what I've thrown away in hard cash to-day I'm apt to call myself some awful hard names, 400,000 dollars is a big pile for a man to light his cigar with. If that gal had only given me herself in exchange, it wouldn't have been a bad bargain. But I dare no more ask that gal to be my wife, than I dare ask Queen Victoria to dance a Cape Cod reel.

Enter Florence, L. 1 E.

Flo What do you mean by doing all these dreadful things?

Asa Which things.

Flo Come here sir. [He does so.]

Asa What's the matter?

Flo Do you know this piece of paper? [Showing burnt paper.]

Asa Well I think I have seen it before. [Aside.] Its old Mark Trenchard's will that I left half burned up like a landhead, that I am.

Flo And you're determined to give up this fortune to Mary Meredith?

Asa Well, I couldn't help it if I tried.

Flo Oh, don't say that.

Asa I didn't mean to do it when I first came here—hadn't the least idea in the world of it, but when I saw that everlasting angel of a gal movin around among them doing fixins like a sunbeam in a shady place; and when I pictured her without a dollar in the world—I—well my old Adam riz right up, and I said, "Asa do it"—and I did it.

Flo Well, I don't know who your old Adam may be, but whoever it is, he's a very honest man to consult you to do so good an action. But how dare you do such an outrageous thing? you impudent—you unceremonious, oh! you unselfish man! you! you, you! [Smothers him with kisses, and runs off, R. 1 E.]

Asa Well, if that ain't worth four hundred thousand dollars, I don't know what is, it was sweeter than sweet cider right out of the bung hole. Let me see how things stand round here. Thanks to old whiskers I've got that ship for the sailor man, and that makes him and Miss Florence all hunk. Then there's that darned old Coyle. Well I guess me and old Murcott can fix his flint for him. Then there's—[Looks off, L.] Christopher Columbus, here comesMary.

Enter Mary, L. 1 E.

Mary Mr. Trenchard, what can I say to you but offer you my lifelong gratitude.

Asa Don't now, Miss, don't—

Mary If I knew what else to offer. Heaven knows there is nothing that is mine to give that I would keep back.

Asa Give me yourself. [Bus.] I know what a rude, ill-mannered block I am; but there's a heart inside me worth something, if it's only for the sake of your dear little image, that's planted right plump in the middle of it.

Mary Asa Trenchard, there is my hand, and my heart is in it.

Asa [Seizes here hand, then drops it suddenly.] Miss Mary, I made what folks call a big sacrifice for you, this morning. Oh! I know it, I ain't so modest, but that I know it. Now what's this you're doing? Is this sacrifice you are making out of gratitude for me? Cause if it is, I wouldn't have it, though not to have it would nigh break my heart, tough as it is.

Mary No, no, I give myself freely to you—as freely as you, this morning, gave my grandfather's property to me.

Asa Say it again, last of hope and blessed promise. [Clasps her in his arms.] Mary, there's something tells me that you'll not repent it. I'm rough, Mary, awful rough, but you needn't fear that I'll ever be rough to you. I've camped out in the woods, Mary, often and often, and seen the bears at play with their cubs in the moonlight, the glistening teeth, that would tear the hunter, was harmless to them; the big strong claws that would peel a man's head, as a knife would a pumpkin, was as soft for them as velvet cushions, and that's what I'll be with you, my own little wife; and if ever harm does come to you, it must come over the dead body of Asa Trenchard.

Mary I know it Asa; and if I do not prove a true and loving wife to you;

may my mother's bright spirit never look down to bless her child.

Asa Wal, if I don't get out in the air, I'll bust. [Exit hastily R. 1 E. pulling Mary after him.]

Enter Binny, L. 1 E. Drunk.

Binny [Calling.] Mr. H'Asa, Mr. H'Asa! Oh he's gone; well, I suppose he'll come back to keep his happointment. Mr. Coyle's quite impatient. It isn't hoften that han hamerican has the run of the wine cellars of Trenchard Manor, and in such company, too. There's me and Mr. Coyle, which is a good judge of old port wine, and he knows it when he drinks; and his clerk, Mr. Murcott, which I don't hexactly like sitting down with clerks. But Mr. H'Asa wished it and Mr. Coyle hadn't any objections, so in course I put my feelings in my pocket, besides, Murcott is a man of hedication, though unfortunately taken to drink. Well, what of that, it's been many a man's misfortune, though I say it, what shouldn't say it, being a butler. But now to join my distinguished party. [Exit, R. 1 E.]

Scene 3.—Wine cellar in 3.

Coyle, Murcott and Binny discovered. Table L., with two cups and bottles. Coyle L. of table, seated. Binny back of table. Murcott sitting on barrel, R. Door in flat with staircase discovered, dark. Stage half dark. Candles on table, lighted.

Coyle A capital glass of wine, Mr. Binny, and a capital place to drink it.

Asa [Without.] Bring a light here, can't you. I've broken my natural allowance of shins already.

Enters D. in F., down stairs.

Asa [To Murcott.] Is he tight yet?

Mur Histered, but not quite gone yet.

Coyle Oh, Mr. Trenchard, glad to see you, to welcome you to the vaults of your ancestors.

Asa Oh! these are the vaults of my ancestors, are they? Wal, you seem to be punishing their spirits pretty well.

Binny Wines, Mr. Asa? The spirits are in the houter cellar.

Coyle Oh, Mr. Asa, there is no place like a wine cellar for a hearty bout. Here you might bawl yourself hoarse beneath these ribs of stone, and nobody hear you. [He shouts and sings very loud.]

Asa Oh, wouldn't they hear you? [Aside.] That's worth knowing.

Binny [Very drunk—rising.] That's right, Mr. Coyle, make as much noise as you like, you are in the cellars of Trenchard Manor, Mr. Coyle. Mr. Coyle, bless you, Mr. Coyle. Mr. Coyle, why his hit Mr. Coyle, I am sitting at the present time, in this present distinguished company? I will tell you, Mr. Coyle, hit his because Hi always hacts and conducts myself has becomes a gentleman, hand Hi knows what's due to manners. [Falls in chair.]

Asa Steady, old hoss, steady.

Binny Hi'm steady. Hi always was steady. [Staggers across to L.H.] Hi'm going to fetch clean glasses. [Exit, L. 3 R.]

Asa Now, Mr. Coyle, suppose you give us a song.

Coyle [Very drunk.] I can't sing, Mr. Trenchard, but I sometimes join in the chorus.

Asa Wal, give us a chorus.

Coyle Will you assist in the vocalization thereof?

Asa [Mimicing.] Will do the best of my endeavors thereunto.

Coyle [Sings.] "We won't go home till morning." Repeat. Repeat [Falls off chair, senseless.]

Asa [Finishing the strain.] "I don't think you'll go home at all." Now, then, quick, Murcott, before the butler comes back, get his keys. [Murcott gets keys from Coyle's pocket and throws them to Asa.] Is this all?

Mur No; the key of his private bureau is on his watch chain, and I can't get it off.

Asa Take watch and all.

Mur No; he will accuse us of robbing him.

Asa Never mind, I'll take the responsibility. [Coyle moves.]

Mur He is getting up.

Asa Well, darn me, knock him down again.

Mur I can't.

Asa Can't you? Well, I can.

[Pulls Murcott away. Knocks Coyle down; is going towards D. in F., meets Binny with tray and glasses; kicks it, knocks Binny down and exits up staircase, followed by Murcott, carrying candle. Dark state. Binny rises; Coyle ditto. Blindly encounter each other and pummel soundly till change.

Quick Change

Scene 4—Chamber in 1, same as Scene 2.

Enter Dundreary and Vernon, L. 1 E. Dundreary stops, C., and is seized with an inclination to sneeze. Motions with his hand to Vernon.

Ver My lord! [Business Dundreary sneezing.] Your lordship! [Dundreary same bus. Louder.] My lord!

Dun There you go; now you've spoiled it.

Ver Spoiled what, my lord?

Dun Spoiled what? why a most magnificent sneeze.

Ver I'm very sorry to interrupt your lordship's sneeze, but I merely wanted to express my gratitude to you for getting me a ship.

Dun Sir, I don't want your gratitude, I only want to sneeze.

Ver Very well, my lord, then I will leave you, and this gives you an opportunity for sneezing. [Crosses to R.] But in return for what you have done for me, should you ever want a service a sailor can offer you, just hail Harry Vernon, and you'll find he'll weigh anchor and be alongside. [Hitches up breeches and exits, R. 1 E.]

Dun Find him alongside? What does he mean by a long side? and he always wants to weigh anchor. What funny fellows the sailors are. Why the devil won't they keep a memorandum of the weight of their anchor? What's the matter with the sailor's side? [Imitates Vernon.] Oh I see, he's got the stomach ache. [Exit, R. 1 E.]

Change Scene

Scene 5—Library in Trenchard Manor in 3 or 4.

Enter Buddicombe, R. 1 E., following Lord Dundreary.

Bud A letter, my lord.

Dun [Takes letter.] You may go. [Exit Buddicombe, R. 1 E. Opens letter.] "My dear Frederick." He calls me Frederick because my name is Robert. "I wrote you on my arrival." Why, I never heard from him. "But I am afraid you didn't get the letter, because I put no name on the envelope." That's the reason why I didn't get it, but who did get it? It must have been some fellow without any name. "My dear brother, the other day a rap came to my door, and some fellows came in and proposed a quiet game of porker." A quiet game of porker, why, they wanted to kill him with a poker. "I consented and got stuck—" Sam's dead, I've got a dead lunatic for a brother—"for the drinks." He got on the other side of the paper, why couldn't he get stuck all on one side. "P. S.—If you don't get this letter let me know, for I shall feel anxious." He's a mad lunatic. [Exit, R. 1 E.]

Change Scene

Scene 6—Coyle's Office in 2. High desk and stool, R. Modern box center against flat. Cabinet, L.

Asa discovered looking over papers on box. Murcott looking in desk.

Asa Have you found it?

Mur No, Mr. Trenchard. I've searched all the drawers but can find no trace of it.

Asa What's this?

Mur That's a cabinet where his father kept old deeds, the key he always carries about him.

Asa Oh, he does, does he? Well I reckon I saw a key as I came in that will open it. [Exit, R. 1 E.]

Mur Key, oh, my poor muddled brain, what can he mean!

Asa [Re-enters with axe.] Here's a key that will open any lock that Hobb ever invented.

Mur Key? what key?

Asa What key, why, Yankee. [Shows axe, begins to break open Cabinet.]

Enter Coyle, R. 2 E.

Coyle Villains! would you rob me?

Mur Stand off, Mr. Coyle, we are desperate. [Now seizes him.]

Asa Here it is a sure as there are snakes in Virginia. Let the old cuss go, Murcott.

Coyle Burglars! oh, you shall dearly pay for this.

Asa Yes, I'll pay—but I guess you'll find the change.

Coyle The law—the law shall aid me.

Asa Wal, perhaps it would be as well not to call in the law just yet. It might look a little further than might be convenient.

Mur It's no use to blunder, Mr. Coyle, you are harmless to us now, for we have that, that will crush you.

Coyle Well, what are your conditions? money, how much?

Asa Wal, we warn't thinking of coming down on your dollars. But you have an appointment with Sir Edward at two, haven't you?

Coyle Well?

Asa Well, I want you to keep that appointment.

Coyle Keep it?

Asa Yes, and that's all I do want you to keep of his, and instead of saying you have come to foreclose the mortgage, I want you to say, you have found the release which proves the mortgage to have been paid off.

Coyle I accept. Is that all?

Asa Not quite. Then I want you to pay off the execution debts.

Coyle What, I pay Sir Edward's debts?

Asa Yes, with Sir Edward's money that stuck to your fingers naturally while passing through your hands.

Coyle [To Murcott.] Traitor!

Mur He knows all, Mr. Coyle.

Coyle Is there anything more!

Asa yes, I want you to apologize to Miss Florence Trenchard, for having the darned impudence to propose for her hand.

Coyle What more?

Asa Then you resign your stewardship in favor of your clerk, Abel Murcott.

Coyle What, that drunkard vagabond?

Asa Well, he was, but he's going to take the pledge at the first pump he comes to.

Mur Yes, I *will* conquer the demon drink, or die in the struggle with him.

Coyle Well, anything more?

Asa Yes, I think the next thing will be to get washed. You're not a handsome man at best, and now you're awful. [Coyle makes a dash at Murcott. Asa catches him and turns him round to R.] Mr. Coyle, in your present state of mind, you had better go first.

Coyle [Bitterly.] Oh, sir, it is your turn now.

Asa Yes, it is my turn, but you can have the first wash. Come along Murcott. [Exeunt, R. 1 E]

Change Scene

Scene 7—Library in Trenchard Manor in 3 or 4.

Sir Edward discovered seated R. of table.

Sir E The clock is on the stroke of two, and Coyle is waiting my decision. In giving her to him, I know I shall be embittering her life to save my fortune, but appearances—no, no, I will not sacrifice her young life so full ofpromise, for a few short years of questionable state for myself, better leave her to the mercy of chance. [Enter Florence, R. U. E.] that sell her to this scoundrel; and to myself, I will not survive the downfall of my house, but end it thus. [Raises pistol to his head. Florence seizes his arm and screams.]

Flo Father, dear father, what despair is this? [Sir Edward buries his face in his hands.] If it is fear of poverty, do not think of me, I will marry this man if I drop dead in my bridal robes.

Enter Binny, R. 1 E.

Binny Mr. Coyle, sir who has come by happointment.

Sir E I will not see him.

Flo Yes, yes, show him up, Mr. Binny. [Exit Binny, R. 1 E.]

Sir E Florence, I will not consent to this sacrifice.

Enter Asa, Coyle and Murcott, R. 1 E.

Sir E How is this Mr. Coyle, you are not alone?

Asa No, you see, squire, Mr. Coyle wishes me and his clerk to witness the cutting off the seals from the mortgage, which he has been lucky enough to find the release of.

Sir E Heavens, is it so?

Coyle Yes, Sir Edward, there is the release executed by my father, which had become detached.

Asa [To him.] Accidentally.

Sir E Saved, saved at last from want!

Coyle Meanwhile I have paid the execution debts out of a find which has just fallen in.

Asa Accidentally. It's astonishing how things have fallen in and out to-day.

Sir E But your demand here? [Points to Florence.]

Coyle I make none, Sir Edward. I regret that I should have conceived so mad a thought; it is enough to unfit me for longer holding position as you agent, which I beg humbly to resign—

Asa [Aside to him.] Recommending as your successor—

Coyle Recommending as my successor Abel Murcott, whose knowledge of your affairs, gained in my office, will render him as useful as I have been.

Asa Yes, just about.

Sir E Your request is granted, Mr. Coyle.

Asa And now, my dear Mr. Coyle, you may a-b-s-q-u-a-t-u-l-a-t-e.

Coyle I go, Sir Edward, with equal good wishes for all assembled here. [Darts a look at Murcott and exits, R. 1 E.]

Asa That's a good man, Sir Edward.

Sir E Yes.

Asa Oh, he's a very good man.

Sir E Yes, he is a good man.

Asa But he can't keep a hotel.

Sir E Mr. Murcott, your offence was heavy.

Flo And so has been his reparation. Forgive him, papa. Mr. Murcott, you saved me; may Heaven bless you.

Mur Yes, I saved her, thank Heaven. I had strength enough for that. [Exits L. 1. E.]

Flo You'll keep your promise and make Mr. Murcott your clerk, papa?

Sir E Yes, I can refuse nothing; I am so happy; I am so happy, I can refuse none anything to-day.

Asa Can't you, Sir Edward! Now, that's awful lucky, for there's two gals want your consent mighty bad.

Sir E Indeed; for what?

Asa To get hitched.

Sir E Hitched?

Asa Yes to get spliced.

Sir E Spliced?

Asa Yes, to get married.

Sir E They have it by anticipation. Who are they?

Asa There's one on 'em. [Points to Florence.]

Sir E Florence! and the other?

Asa She's right outside. [Exit, hastily, R. 1. E.]

Sir E Well, and who is the happy man, Lord Dun—

Flo Lord Dundreary! No, papa—but Harry Vernon. He's not poor now, though he's got a ship.

Re-enter Asa, with Mary.

Asa Here's the other one, Sir Edward.

Sir E Mary? Who is the object of your choice?

Mary Rough-spun, honest-hearted Asa Trenchard.

Sir E Ah! Mr. Trenchard you win a heart of gold.

Flo And so does Mary, papa, believe me. [Crosses to Asa. Mary and Sir Edward go up.]

Flo What's the matter?

Asa You make me blush.

Flo I don't see you blushing.

Asa I'm blushing all the way down my back.

Flo Oh, you go long. [Goes up stage.]

Asa Hello! here's all the folks coming two by two, as if they were pairing for Noah's ark. Here's Mrs. Mountchestnut and the Sailor man. [Enter as Asa calls them off.] Here's De Boots and his gal, and darn me, if here ain't old setidy fetch it, and the sick gal, how are you buttons? [Dundreary knocks against Asa, who is in C. of stage.]

Dun There's that damned rhinocerous again. [Crosses to L. with Georgina, and seats her.]

Asa Here comes turkey cock, number two, and his gal, and darn me, if here ain't Puffy and his gal.

Sir E Mr. Vernon, take her, she's yours, though Heaven knows what I shall do without her.

Mrs M [Rising.] Ah, Sir Edward, that is just my case; but you'll never know what it is to be a mother. [Comes down, L. C.] Georgina, Augusta, my dears, come here. [They come down each side of her.] You'll sometimes think of your poor mamma, bless you. [Aside to them.] Oh, you couple of fools.

[Bumps their foreheads. Dundreary has business with Georgina, then leads her to a seat, L.]

De B [To Dundreary.] Why, Fred, we're all getting married!

Dun Yes, it's catching, like the cholera.

Binny I 'ope, Sir Edward, there's no objections to my leading Miss Sharpe to the hymenial halter.

Sir E Certainly not, Mr. Binny.

Bud [To Dun.] And Skillet and I have made so bold, My lord—

Dun Yes, you generally do make bold—but bless you, my children—bless you.

Asa Say, you, lord, buttons, I say, whiskers.

Dun Illustrious exile? [Comes down.]

Asa They're a nice color, ain't they?

Dun Yes, they're all wight now.

Asa All wight? no, they're all black.

Dun When I say wight I mean black.

Asa Say, shall I tell that sick gal about that hair dye?

Dun No, you needn't tell that sick gal about that hair dye!

Asa Wal, I won't, if you don't want me to.

Dun [Aside.] That man is a damned rattlesnake.

[Goes up, sits in Georgina's lap—turns to apologize, sits in Augusta's lap—same business with Mrs. M, then goes back to Georgina.]

Asa Miss Georgina. [She comes down.] How's your appetite? shall I tell that lord about the beefsteak and onions I saw you pitching into?

Geo Please don't, Mr. Trenchard, I'm so delicate.

Asa Wal, I won't, if you don't want me to.

Geo Oh, thank you.

[Backs up stage and sits in Dundreary's lap, who has taken her seat.]

Asa Miss Gusty. [Augusta comes down.] Got your boots, hain't you?

Aug Yes, Mr. Trenchard.

Asa How do they fit you? Say, shall I tell that fellow you were after me first?

Aug [Extravagantly.] Not for the world, Mr. Trenchard.

Asa [Mimicing.] Wal, I won't, if you don't want me to.

Asa [To Mrs M.] Mrs. Mountchestnut.

Dun [Coming down.] Sir, I haven't a chestnut to offer you, but if you'd like some of your native food, I'll order you a doughnut?

Asa I dough not see it.

Dun [Laughs.] That's good.

Asa Yes, very good.

Dun For you.

Asa Oh, you get out, I mean the old lady.

Dun Mrs. Mountchessington, this illustrious exile wishes to see you. [Mrs M. comes down.]

Asa Wal, old woman?

Mrs M Old woman, sir?

Asa Got two of them gals off your hands, haven't you?

Mrs M I'm proud to say, I have.

Asa Shall I tell them fellows you tried to stick them on me first?

Mrs M You'll please not mention the subject.

Asa Wal, I won't, if you don't want me to. [Backs up;—curtseying;—knocks back against Dundreary, who is stooping to pick up a handkerchief. They turn and bunk foreheads.] Say, Mr. Puffy. [Binny comes down.] Shall I tell Sir Edward about your getting drunk in the wine cellar?

Binny You need not—not if you don't like unto.

Asa Wal, I won't, if you don't want me to.

Binny Remember the hold hadage. "A still tongue shows a wise ead."

Asa X Q's me.

Binny O, I, C. [Goes up.]

Flo [Comes down, L.] Well cousin, what have you to say to us? [Mary comes down R. of Asa.]

Asa Wal, I ain't got no ring, to put in your noses, but I's got one to put on your finger. [To Mary.] And I guess the sailor man has one to put on yours, and I guess you two are as happy as clams at high water.

Flo I am sure you must be very happy.

Asa Wal, I am not so sure about my happiness.

Flo Why, you ungrateful fellow. What do want to complete it?

Asa [To Audience.] My happiness depends on you.

Flo And I am sure you will not regret your kindness shown to Our American Cousin. But don't go yet, pray—for Lord Dundreary has a word to say. [Calls Dundreary.]

Dun [Sneezes.] That's the idea.

CURTAIN

www.ingramcontent.com/pod-product-compliance
Lightning Source LLC
Chambersburg PA
CBHW060800310726
48980CB00002B/176
* 9 7 8 3 7 3 2 6 2 7 5 6 1 *